I0743426

She's a witch, but no spell or potion can help her now…

White witch Kole Trillion's life is perfect—almost. She has a successful business, customers who swear by her potions and spells, a black cat named Boo as a familiar, and a number of loyal friends. Unfortunately, she also has the bad luck to fall in love with a man who hates her. Unable to device a spell or potion to help her out of her distressing predicament, Kole's determined not to let it ruin her life. And to keep her embarrassing heartache her own dark, little secret. But when Cupid gets involved, all bets are off.

He's a cop who doesn't believe in magic—or in love…

Police Detective Gage Corwin is convinced Kole's nothing but a con artist out to cheat the public. Determined to put her out of business, Gage launches an investigation to prove she's a fraud and a criminal. But the evidence just doesn't add up. Not only can't he find anyone she's cheated, he can't find a logical explanation for the things that are happening to his life—or his heart. But when he unwittingly mocks Cupid, the whole thing blows up in Gage's face.

Books by Pepper O'Neal

Love Potion No. 2-14

Blood Fest Series

Blood Fest: Chasing Destiny

Blood Fest: Cursing Fate

Black Ops Chronicles Series

Black Ops Chronicles: Dead Run

Black Ops Chronicles: Dead Men Don't

Love Potion No. 2-14

Pepper O'Neal

A CIBOLA PRESS PUBLICATION

To Boo

Chapter 1

A note from Cupid's diary:

In my opinion, these subjects needed a hand from me because Kole Trillion was Detective Gage Corwin's prime suspect in a fraud case. He accused her of being a con artist and fleecing the customers of her shop. He absolutely refused to believe she was really a witch. And a good witch? Not a chance!

To be honest, at first I only focused on them because Trillion issued me a challenge—not that she realized it—and I've never been able to resist a dare. Though, on second thought, I probably would've targeted them eventually, because Corwin was such a hardass.

Humans! What a joke they are. They think just because they live in what they call the "twenty-first century," it's acceptable to be cynical and scientifically minded. They don't even believe in magic anymore.

The other gods tell me this is something I have to accept, I should be used to it by now, I need to just deal with it and blah, blah, blah, ad infinitum.

To them I say: get real! I may have to live with the humans' lack of faith, but I don't have to like it. So when I got the chance for a little payback on Corwin—well, what was I supposed to do? And although they might not admit it, all the other gods would've done exactly the same thing.

Corwin not only didn't believe in magic, he didn't believe in love. Which meant the arrogant fool didn't believe in *me*. And that really stuck in my craw. On top of that, he had the audacity to laugh at me. Which, as any god will tell you, is going just a bit too far.

Normally, I'm an easy-going, fun-loving god. But when that narrow-minded, hard-headed, bigoted son-of-a—er, oops. Sorry. Got carried away for a moment. Gods aren't supposed to swear. It lacks class. And I probably shouldn't have used that particular phrase, anyway. It isn't really offensive enough to describe the jerk, and I wouldn't want to insult the gods' best friends by comparing them with someone like Gage Corwin.

But I'm getting off the track here. I didn't shoot Trillion. I didn't need to. The silly little fool was already in love with Corwin. Poor thing.

I also didn't shoot Corwin—at first. I figured that, in all fairness, I should see if he and Trillion would connect on their own. So before I shot him, I clobbered him over the head with my bow and gave him a monster headache, trying to make him go to Trillion's Magic Closet for help. It took him three days, but he went.

Who knows, it might even have worked. However, when he laughed at me…well. as they say in the twenty-first century, "all bets are off."

Served him right, too. Didn't believe in love? Hah! I guess I showed him.

Chapter 2

A small shop in Morro Bay, California, on a Sunday afternoon in early January:

I'm sorry, Kole, but he's doing it again."

Alarmed by the anxiety in her assistant's voice, Kole dropped her clipboard and spun around. She scanned the interior of her shop but saw nothing amiss. "Geeze, Lynn, can't you be a little more specific?" Exasperated, she knelt to retrieve her scattered papers. "You sound just like one of my nephews tattling on his brothers," she said, fishing for wayward pages under the shelves.

She straightened up, documents in hand, and began putting her inventory sheets back in order. "And like my sister always tells them, 'if I don't know who you're referring to, I can't do much about whatever he's doing again.'"

"I'm talking about that awful cop. He's sitting on the hood of his car outside, shooting dirty looks at our store."

Kole glanced out the window. Sure enough, there sat Detective Gage Corwin. And every gorgeous inch of the six-foot hunk looked hard and implacable. She suffered a sharp pang of longing as he raked his hands through his thick chestnut hair and shifted his exceptionally fine ass to another spot on the car. "Has he been here long?"

Lynn hesitated. "Almost an hour. I didn't say anything earlier because I hoped he'd go away before you realized he was out there. I'm sorry," she repeated when Kole opened her mouth to protest. "I just hate how his attitude hurts your feelings." She walked over and rubbed a comforting hand down Kole's back. "But since the bastard isn't leaving, I figured I'd better tell you."

The scowl on Gage's chiseled face did more than just hurt Kole's feelings. It gouged holes in her heart that bled her emotions dry.

"Has he been questioning all our customers again?"

"No, not all of them this time. Just the women."

"Maybe he's looking for a date." Forcing herself to ignore the pain, Kole went back to checking her stock of love potions.

"Oh, sure. Like, he really wants to date anyone who buys products from *you*. He thinks you're evil, Kole. A true daughter of Satan." When Kole chuckled, Lynn sighed. "Okay, maybe that's a little strong. But he definitely sees you as a charlatan and a fraud. A criminal." Bristling with indignation, she tapped her foot on the pale stone floor. "The man has no respect for you or for magic." With her hands fisted on her hips, she glared out the window at Gage. "He's a menace, Kole. Why you don't just put a spell on him? Or slip him a potion—anything to make him go away and leave us alone?"

"Because the first law of white magic is to harm none." And because her foolish heart had it bad for the mouthwatering detective. But Kole was determined to keep that dirty little secret to herself.

"What about the damage he's doing to us?" Lynn demanded.

Kole swallowed a laugh. Like a dog with its proverbial bone, her assistant just couldn't let go. Shaking her head, Kole concentrated on her inventory and let the woman rant.

"Our customers don't like being interrogated every time they come here, and a lot of them are staying away." Lynn waved a hand around the store. "We've only had a dozen customers since noon. Even our online sales are dropping."

"Oh, come on, Lynn. That's not Detective Corwin's fault." Kole picked up a bright red bottle of Love Potion Two-Fourteen and frowned. The magic was fading. "Been on the shelf too long," she muttered. "Needs recharging." She looked over at Lynn. "You know as well as I do business is always slow this time of year. After Christmas, people take a break from the crowds and shopping. Things'll pick up again by Valentine's Day." Slipping the love potion into the pocket of her jeans, she marked its status on the inventory. "Don't worry. Our customers are loyal. They always come back."

"Not if that fricking cop has his way." Lynn's lips curved into a sly grin. "You know what you need to do, don't you?" She didn't wait for an answer. "You need to slip him some love potion. That'd fix his wagon. He'd be so crazy about you, he'd be willing to do anything for you. Even if what you ask is for him to just leave you alone."

Kole laughed. "You can't be serious." When Lynn nodded, she groaned. "Haven't you heard *anything* I tell my customers? Love potions can't force a man to love you. They can't take away someone's choice. The spell doesn't even work unless there's already some affection between the two people involved. And then it only lasts for seventy-two hours. After that, the couple's on their own." Finished with the love potions, she moved on to the health remedies. "It doesn't have any effect on strangers. And it *certainly* won't work on enemies."

She paused, sensing a presence close by. But when she looked around, all she saw was Gage, still leaning against his car, his striking amber eyes glaring at her store, his full, sensuous lips pressed into a hard, thin line. Was it just his negative emotions she'd felt?

She shook off her unease, telling herself she was just being paranoid. "And in case you hadn't noticed, Lynn, that man out there really hates me."

Lynn's shoulders drooped. "You're probably right," she said, her words coming out in a huff. "Too bad there isn't really a Cupid with his magic bow and arrow. Corwin would make the perfect target."

Kole winced. She knew there *was* a Cupid—and her heart would love to have the little god aim an arrow with her name on it at Gage. But her head knew better. Cupid was a capricious god, and he didn't take requests from mortals. Not that she'd ever ask. She wouldn't really want Gage to love her unless he chose to do so of his own free will. And that would never happen.

"While it pains me to admit it," she said, "the man despises me so much, I doubt Cupid's arrow would have any more effect on his granite heart than my love potions would." She fought back the tears that threatened to give her away, disgusted with herself for letting Gage get to her like this. "After all, Cupid's not a very big god, and I can't imagine he'd be powerful enough to overcome all the hostile male aggression that makes up Detective Corwin. Besides—"

She glanced over in surprise as the bell on the shop door jingled. Strange. The door hadn't opened. And the windows were closed, so there wasn't any breeze. Only she and Lynn were in the shop, and neither of them had gone near the front door. So who, or what, rang the bell?

A sudden chill skated down her spine, and she trembled with the knowledge that her life was about to change. Irrevocably. She squeezed her eyes shut in dismay. Although she hadn't gotten a sense of dread to go with the premonition—this time—she was too much of a realist to believe that whatever was coming might be a change for the better.

Her life just didn't work that way.

Chapter 3

Gage raked his hands through his hair then shifted his body against the fender of his car, trying to find a more comfortable position. Not that there was one. Sighing, he rubbed at the tension in the back of his neck.

What the hell was he even doing here? On one of his rare Sundays off work he should be home catching the game on television. Or down at his favorite watering hole. Hell, anyplace but here. So why was he giving himself a sore ass trying to interrogate the customers of Trillion's Magic Closet? *Because the woman's a crook, you dumbass. That's why.* Gage knew it. *Knew* Kole was a fraud and a con artist. He just couldn't prove it. Yet.

She posed as a witch—a white witch, of course. Gage rolled his eyes. Obviously the woman knew people would assume white magic was better than black. *As if any type of magic even exists.* It amazed him that so many people in this day and age swallowed such hogwash.

Kole sold *love potions*, for Pete's sake. And people not only bought them, they claimed the damned things worked! As hard as he'd tried to pin down a single dissatisfied patron in Kole's steady stream of customers, not one of them would admit to being hoodwinked. Instead, they kept coming back for more. And they insisted she was the real deal—a good witch.

Yeah, right. Oh, he didn't doubt she was a witch, but just the kind that brewed up evil schemes to separate naïve fools from their money. She had to be one hell of an actress, though. She'd conned even his normally shrewd and sharp-minded partner, Jeff Fox. And that wasn't easy. Gage might've been impressed—if he hadn't been so angry.

Frustrated, he jammed his hands into his pockets. Jeff was now married to Missy, a woman who'd actually confessed she'd used one of Kole's love potions on him.

Not only did Jeff claim to love the conniving wench, he swore up and down the so-called magic potion had worked for three days and then worn off. And when it did, he realized he was in love with Missy and had been for months.

"Missy." Gage snorted. "What kind of a name is *Missy?*"

She had to be in league with Kole. The two of them must have planned the whole thing. But how could his levelheaded partner have fallen for such an obvious con?

People could be incredibly gullible. Or maybe they were just too embarrassed to admit they'd been taken. He'd have gone with door number two, except none of Kole's customers seemed the least bit embarrassed. Not even Jeff.

Gage could have understood it if it had just been the men who refused to cooperate with his investigation. Kole was a real looker. No question. With her lime-green eyes, abundant red hair, luscious curves, and mile-long legs, she didn't need witchcraft to charm a man. Hell, the very thought of her filled Gage with lust. But women could usually see right through other females. So why did they defend her, too?

He heaved another sigh and levered himself off the fender. Accosting her customers in front of the shop wasn't getting him anywhere. He'd wasted over an hour already today and accomplished nothing. But he'd get her. He'd subpoena her customer list and interview every damn one of them in their homes until he found one who'd admit to being conned. Then he'd convince whoever it was to press charges.

He reached for the driver-side door handle then jerked back as an enormous house cat jumped on the hood of the car, landing with a thud.

"Hey! Get off my ride, you big oaf." Big was almost an understatement, since the animal probably weighed twenty-five pounds. "Shit, what're they feeding you?" he growled, checking his hood for dents. "Stray dogs and small children?"

With a twitch of its tail, the pure black creature strutted across the hood, up the windshield, and onto the roof, leaving a trail of muddy paw prints in its wake.

"Figures." Gage shook his head. "After all, I just washed the damn thing."

He cursed and fisted his hands on his hips, trying to look intimidating.

The cat responded by sitting on its haunches, curling its tail around its feet, and glaring at him with its evil-looking yellow eyes.

"Where the hell did you come from, anyway? And how'd you get mud on your paws to track all over my car? It hasn't rained for days."

He made a grab for the little monster, but it scooted just out of reach, sat down again, and winked one golden eye.

"Get off my car, you dumb piece of shit," he shouted. "Or I'll pull out my gun and blow your worthless ass away."

"No, don't hurt him!"

Gage spun around as Kole rushed out of her store, her beautiful green eyes filled with horror.

"Shit." He hung his head and pinched the bridge of his nose with his thumb and forefinger. *I should have known. A cat this ornery could only belong to her.* "I wasn't going to shoot your cat," he muttered, raising his hands to show her they were empty. "I was just trying to scare him off my car."

"Boo's not *my* cat," she declared indignantly. "He's a familiar. So save your threats and bullying. They won't have any effect on him."

"Boo, huh?" Gage snorted. "Should've guessed. What else would a witch call her black cat?" Taking a deep breath, he struggled to control his temper—and his libido. "So then, if my methods won't work, what would you suggest for getting this behemoth off my car? You wouldn't happen to have a *broom* I could borrow, would you?"

"Cute." Her voice was ripe with sarcasm. "I don't suppose it occurred to you to try asking nicely."

"You're joking, right? You seriously think dipshit will leave just because I make it a request instead of an order?"

"You'll never know unless you try. Of course, if it's too much of a strain on your ego to ask politely, you could just wait until he decides to move on his own. But I warn you, that might take hours," she said with a smirk. "And his name's Boo, not dipshit."

"Whatever." *Might as well humor her*, he decided. He turned back to the cat. "If it's not too much trouble, Boo," he said, giving him a small bow, "could you *please* get your fat ass off my car?" Glancing over his shoulder at Kole, he added, "Sorry, but that's about as polite as I can manage without—"

Movement out of the corner of his eye drew his attention back to Boo. The beast stood up, yawned, stretched, and walked regally back down the windshield to the hood. Then he jumped to the ground and sauntered over to Kole.

"Way to go, Boo," she whispered, picking him up and nuzzling him. With the cat in her arms, she headed back to the shop, pausing on the threshold. "You're welcome to come in and check out my store, Detective, if you think it will help with your investigation."

"Yeah, right," he scoffed. "I'm sure you're smart enough not to make an offer like that unless you've already destroyed all the incriminating evidence."

Heat flared in her eyes, igniting a fire in Gage's loins.

"There wasn't any incriminating evidence in the first place." Her face hardened. "Investigate all you want, Detective. But be careful how you do it. If you harass my customers too much, I can't be responsible for the consequences."

"Oh boy, I'm really shaking in my boots now." He gave a mock shudder. "What are you going to do, turn me into a toad?"

"Well, I would," she said, with the barest hint of triumph in her smile. "But somebody obviously beat me to it." With that, she stepped into the store and closed the door firmly behind her.

"Ouch. Guess she won that battle," he muttered as he got into his car to drive home. "But the war isn't over yet."

Kole may have covered up her crimes well, but the evidence against her had to be out there somewhere. And he'd find it. Soon.

Chapter 4

Two weeks later:

Gage sat at his desk in the police station, staring at his notes and cursing the headache that had been tormenting him for three long days.

"Hey, Corwin." Jeff plopped down in a chair beside the desk. "You don't look so good, pal."

Gage glowered at his partner. "Got a headache that won't go away. Feels like someone clobbered me on the head with a blunt instrument."

"You know what you need to do?"

"Yeah. Decapitate myself."

Jeff chuckled. "No, dumbass. Head over to Trillion's Magic Closet and get one of her headache potions. Those things work miracles for me."

"Now look, Fox." Gage banged a hand down on his desk then winced as the noise rammed into his skull like a pile driver. "You may be willing to buy that woman's bullshit, but that doesn't mean I will. She's nothing but a crook."

"Uh-huh." Jeff grinned and pointed at Gage's notes. "So tell me this: did you find even one person yet who admits to buying a product from her that doesn't work?"

"No, and I can't understand it." Gage lowered his head and rapped it twice—very gently—against the desktop. "People usually get pissed when they get ripped off. What's the damned woman doing, hypnotizing them so they think her products work?"

"Why don't you go find out?"

"What the hell do you think I've been trying to do?" Gage picked up a handful of papers and shook them at Jeff. "Just listen to what her idiotic customers have to say. 'Her headache potions have cured my migraines completely,'" he quoted, reading from his notes. "'I've thrown away all my prescription pain killers.' Or this. 'Kole Trillion's a lifesaver. Since I used her love potion on my husband, he no longer wants a divorce.

He's given up his mistress and come back to me. We've never been happier.' Or—wait a minute. Let me find it." He searched through the pages. "Here it is. Listen to this. 'Her arthritis potion cured my fingers instantly, and now I can knit a sweater for my new grandson without any pain at all. It's just like getting brand new hands.'" Massaging his temples, he groaned. "'Brand new hands.' And the dumb woman didn't stop knitting the whole time I was there. I just don't get it."

"I think you get it fine," Jeff said with a sigh. "You just don't like what your evidence tells you: the woman does only good."

"She doesn't do any good at all." Gage waved the notes again. "These people only think she does."

"Face it, partner, if whatever Kole gave those people made one able to get by without prescription pain meds, had another's husband canceling plans for a divorce, and gave a third her life back, how can you say she hasn't done good and still call yourself a detective?"

"Because it's a *lie*, dammit!" Gage could only shake his head that a shrewd cop like Jeff would even consider such nonsense. "There's no such thing as magic. And you should know it."

"What *I* know is irrelevant, since you refuse to listen to me. Besides, whether magic really exists isn't the issue here. The question is whether or not Kole's doing something illegal. So find out. Get a warrant and subpoena her books. And get some of her products for testing."

"I tried. I got a warrant for the customer list, but the judge wouldn't give me anything else. Said I didn't have probable cause."

"Yeah, kinda hard to make a case for fraud when the woman has only satisfied customers." With another sigh, Jeff got to his feet. "And since you're too much of a pussy to do what needs to be done, you're bound to keep spinning your wheels and getting nowhere."

"Wait just a damn minute!" Gage grabbed Jeff's arm before he could leave. "What the hell are you talking about?"

Jeff jerked free of Gage's grasp then leaned down and placed both palms flat on the desk, his face inches from Gage's nose. "You've got a major headache, you imbecile. Go to Trillion's and buy a headache potion. In fact, buy two. Turn one bottle over to the lab and get them to tell you what's in it. But first, drink the other one as medicine for your headache. If it doesn't work for you, well then, you've got your dissatisfied customer: you." He straightened, crossed his arms over his chest, and grinned at Gage. "But if it *does* work, give up this idiotic crusade and leave the woman alone. But I'm betting you're too much of a wimp to try the second half of that. Because then you'd have to admit you're wrong about her. Hell, you might even have to face the fact that you have feelings for her. And that just scares the shit out of you, doesn't it?"

"You're crazy." Gage leaned back in his chair, trying to put some distance between them. "I only want to get a dangerous criminal off the streets." Even before he'd finished speaking, he realized how lame his words sounded, so he wasn't surprised when Jeff burst out laughing.

"Dangerous criminal. Right. There's really something evil about a woman who sells tonics that do nothing but help people."

"How can you say that? After Missy admitted she used a love potion on you?"

"Because it's the best thing that ever happened to me, that's why. And if I hadn't been such an idiot in the first place, Missy wouldn't have found it necessary. So Kole Trillion will only get praise from me. You're all alone on this one, pal." He turned and headed off, calling back over his shoulder. "Let me know if you get the guts to take my challenge."

"I'm not afraid to go buy a damn potion," Gage muttered, glaring at Jeff's retreating back.

Chapter 5

His headache had him seeing double, so Gage took a cab to Trillion's. The trip lasted fifteen minutes, and he spent the whole time reassuring himself Jeff was way off base. This wasn't an idiotic crusade. And the only feelings he had for Kole were those of a cop for his suspect—distrust and disgust, coupled with the desire to put a heartless con artist out of business. By the time he got to the shop, he was almost convinced.

He started toward Kole's front door then hesitated. Maybe this wasn't such a good idea. He didn't have a clue how to approach her. How could he get her to give him access to her books? Should he bluff, make her think he had a warrant? Or forget the books and just buy some potions to take to the lab? If the lab guys came up with anything he could use, would it be enough for a warrant? No, probably not. Unless they found something harmful, which he didn't really expect. Otherwise, she'd have a slew of sick and dying customers.

Impeded by the sledgehammers pounding away at his brain, he couldn't come up with a viable plan. He turned around, intending to go back to the station. But the cab had already driven off. Shit. *Guess I'll just have to play it by ear*. Squaring his shoulders, he took a deep breath and entered the store.

Kole stood at the counter, ringing up a sale. She glanced over as the door opened. Her eyes widened. The little bottle she was holding slipped from her fingers and smashed on the counter. Pieces of pink glass floated on a pool of yellow liquid spreading rapidly across the countertop.

"Oh, no, I'm so sorry," she told the customer. She pulled a roll of paper towels from a cabinet behind her. "It didn't splash on your clothes, did it?"

"No, no. I'm fine. Don't worry about it."

"Lynn," Kole called out.

"What's the matter?" asked the short, perky brunette who scurried out of the back room. She stopped dead, staring at Gage. "What's *he* doing here?"

"Never mind that." Kole scooped up glass and liquid in a wad of paper towels. "Get Mrs. Thompson another bottle of potion." She dumped the sopping mess in a trashcan and pulled off another string of towels. "Headache Potion Six-Eighteen."

"Right." Lynn stomped over to a shelf, came back with a bottle, and handed it to Kole. "I'll take care of him," she said, jerking her thumb in Gage's direction.

"No. You finish ringing up this sale. I'll see what he wants."

"Kole—"

"Don't argue, Lynn. I'll be fine."

"You'd better be." Her mouth set in a firm, tight line, Lynn walked behind the counter. "Just shout if you need backup."

Kole patted Lynn's arm then murmured something to Mrs. Thompson before turning to Gage. "Well, Detective. This is quite a surprise. I didn't think you cared for my shop."

"I don't. I—" Lights flashed behind his eyes, making him dizzy. The pain in his head doubled. He groaned. His hands flew to his temples as he staggered backward.

Chapter 6

G age!"

He heard Kole's voice as if from a distance. The concern in it surprised him. He'd given the woman no reason to care about him.

Feeling her body suddenly much too close to his, he blinked and looked down. She had her arms around him and was easing him into a chair by the door. Her hair tickled his cheek. The scent of wildflowers and honey filled his nostrils. Man, she smelled good. And her touch felt like heaven. Panicked, he jerked away from her and slumped down in the chair.

"Just rest here a minute," she said. "Lynn, will you

please make Detective Corwin a cup of jasmine tea?"

"Only if I can add hemlock."

"Behave yourself, Lynn." Kole gave Gage an apologetic smile. "My assistant's a little overprotective, I'm afraid. But don't worry. We're fresh out of hemlock." She knelt and studied his eyes. "How long have you had this headache?"

"How did you know I have a headache?" he asked, suspicious. "Jeff called you, didn't he?"

She sighed. "No one called me. I can see the pain in your eyes." Rising, she placed he hand on his forehead. To his amazed relief, the pain lessened to almost bearable. "How long?" she repeated.

"Three days." He closed his eyes and leaned into her hand, wondering why it felt so good against his skin. "It's nothing serious. Just the pressures of the job."

"Uh-huh. Well, tension headache or not, I imagine it's still very painful."

Her fingers slipped around to massage the back of his neck. His pain eased a little more. *How the hell does she do that?*

"Sit tight a minute," she ordered, withdrawing her hand.

He blinked his eyes open and stifled a moan at the sudden loss of her touch.

Don't make a fool of yourself, dumbass.

But he had to stop himself from reaching for her.

She crossed the shop to a shelf stocked with small, colorful bottles. Selecting a bright blue one, she hurried back and held it out to him.

He took it, eyeing it warily. "What's this?"

"It's a headache potion. A combination of herbs and…stuff. It'll make you feel better." Her smile made his breath catch. "No hemlock. I promise."

He had no problem with the herbs. It was the "and stuff" that concerned him. "In other words, it's one of your *magic* potions."

She squared her shoulders. "Herbs have been used in healing for centuries, Detective."

Her voice had turned cool. Gage couldn't explain why he suddenly despised himself for causing that aloof tone. He'd liked it much better when she'd called him by his first name.

She tapped the bottle. "It's a proven method of treating many health problems. Including headaches."

"Proven, huh? Okay, okay," he added when he saw those gorgeous eyes spark with indignation. "I suppose there's some validity to herbs in healing."

Mrs. Thompson came up and peered over Kole's shoulder. "Oh, that's a wonderful potion. That'll fix you right up, young man. Don't you worry." She beamed at

Kole. "This girl's a real miracle worker. Her stuff always does wonders for me."

Gage wished they'd stop calling it "stuff." The word could mean anything.

"Thanks, Mrs. Thompson," Kole said. "You have a nice day, now." She nudged her customer out the front door just as Lynn walked up with the tea.

"Here, let me have that." Kole took the mug from her assistant. Probably afraid the woman would dump it in his lap. After sending Lynn off to finish what she was doing in the back room, Kole reached out a hand for the bottle Gage held. "It's up to you, Detective. But I promise you, there is nothing in that potion that can harm you."

He turned the pretty little container in the sunlight streaming through the window. The prism effect of sun on glass made blue highlights dance on the beige stone floor. What the hell, if the potion made him sick, he'd have the evidence he needed to bring a case against Kole. With a sigh, he handed her the bottle and watched her pour the potion into the tea. When she gave him the mug, the invigorating aroma of jasmine and honeysuckle bathed in fresh mountain sunshine had him inhaling deeply. He hesitated then took a testing sip. Delicious. Greedily, he drank down the rest of it. By the last swallow, his headache had vanished.

"Thanks," he said in amazement.

"No problem. But I doubt you came in here for a headache cure, did you?"

Finding himself unable to bluff, he shook his head. "Not exactly. But I appreciate it all the same."

"Why did you come in?"

"I—I wanted some, ah, I mean, I wanted to get, ah, some—some of your potions." Why the hell was he stuttering? He never stuttered. Shaking his head, he concentrated on the mission. "To buy some. Some potions, I mean."

She blinked. "Why? You don't believe in magic."

"Is that a requirement before someone's allowed to be a customer?"

"Look, Detective, I see little point in wasting my time or your money. So why don't you tell me what you're really after?"

The sadness and resignation in her voice made him feel like an ass. Cursing himself for softening toward her, he chanted in his mind: *She's a fraud and doesn't deserve my sympathy.*

Yes, his headache was gone, but that could have been just the hot tea easing his tension. Or maybe it was the herbs in the potion. It didn't mean she wasn't doing more harm than good. So why not just tell her what he wanted and see what her reaction was?

"I thought I'd take some of your products into the lab and make sure there's nothing harmful in them." He leaned his head against the back of his chair and gazed up at her. "And I'd like to review your financial records." He thought he saw a flicker of pain in her eyes, but it vanished so fast, he told himself he imagined it. Nevertheless, he felt compelled to give her an out. "I don't have a warrant."

With another sigh, she nodded. "I imagine a warrant is hard to get when my customers swear by my products." Beckoning with a finger, she headed across the shop to a row of shelves. "Love potions start here," she said, pointing to the top shelf, "and go to there." Her gesture encompassed four rows of five bottles each. "Health remedies are from there on over. On the lower shelves, you'll find ones for various other needs." She picked up a small golden jar from the health section and handed it to him. "You can see by the label on the back what the potion is designed to do."

Gage read the information on the bottle. The concoction it held was intended for indigestion, gastritis, colitis, and stomach flu. "Isn't this practicing medicine without a license?" he asked, brandishing the jar.

Her chin came up. "Sorry, Detective, but you'll have to try a little harder to find something to use against me." She waved her hand at a group of framed certificates on the wall behind the cash register. "As you can see, I am a trained, certified, and fully-licensed herbalist. I'm in compliance with all state and federal regulations for preparing, labeling, and selling my products."

"Yes, I know."

Her eyes narrowed. "Of course. You'd have discovered my credentials in your investigation of me, wouldn't you? And yet you still refuse to give up."

Gage watched in fascination as her eyes iced over. How could such a warm shade of green turn so cold and brittle? He shivered when she locked that frigid gaze with his.

"Take whatever you want. It's on the house." Her shoulders straight and her head held high, she marched back to the checkout counter, calling over her shoulder. "I'll make you a copy of my books."

"Kole, no!" Lynn rushed out of the back room. "You don't have to do that unless he has a warrant." She glared over at Gage. "And you don't, do you?"

Before he could answer, Kole put her hand on Lynn's arm. "It's all right. He doesn't need a warrant. I'm willing to cooperate fully with the detective's investigation."

"But why should you?" Lynn demanded.

"Why shouldn't I?" Kole pressed a switch on a

computer sitting on the shelf behind the cash register and pulled a CD out of a cupboard. "I have absolutely nothing to hide."

"I know that, but even so—"

"Even so, if Detective Corwin has questions, I'm happy to answer them." Kole shot him another freezing look. "Maybe then, he'll leave me the hell alone."

Chapter 7

Kole watched Gage get into a cab, carrying a sack containing ten bottles of potion and the CD she'd given him. Tears stung her eyes. Cursing, she blinked them away. How could she have been so stupid as to fall in love with a man who hated her? A man who thought she personified evil?

Her mind flashed back to the first time she'd met him. It had been at Jeff and Missy's wedding reception. He'd been arrogant and rude, accusing her of helping Missy in some kind of scheme to con Jeff.

When she'd retorted that she'd never even met Jeff before that night and knew Missy only as a customer, he'd dismissed her claims with a snort. And when she asked him what possible motive they could have for trying to con Jeff—an underpaid police detective, for crying out loud—he'd muttered something about all women being witches…or was it bitches?…and how they hardly needed a reason to con a man.

Any sane witch would have used a repelling spell to make the man leave her alone. But something about Gage's eyes had stopped her. The man had such captivating amber eyes—intense, piercing, and brimming with so much unhappiness she couldn't bear to use her magic against him. So what had she done instead? She'd tripped on her heart and sprawled at his feet. Man, what a fool she was. Maybe she deserved all the pain he'd given her.

Shaking her head at her own stupidity, she walked over to straighten the mess Gage had made of her shelves. As she lined up the bottles back into neat little rows, a heavy thud on the ledge outside the window sent her scrambling backward. Then a huge black paw scraped its claws across the glass, setting her nerves on edge.

She scrunched her eyes closed and shuddered as Boo scraped the windowpane again, announcing his arrival with his usual panache.

She should have known he'd show up. Though how

he always seemed to sense when she was hurting was a mystery to her. Must have something to do with magic. Or with familiars. She opened her eyes and stared through the glass into his huge yellow ones.

"I supposed you want in." She saw Boo's mouth move, heard the faint meow. Of course, he wanted in. Pushing the window open, she stepped back to give him some maneuvering room. "It's a wonder you manage to balance your fat ass on that skinny ledge," she said as he soared gracefully through the window and over the shelves. He landed on the floor beside her and stared up at her with narrowed eyes.

"Don't look at me like that," she scolded, pulling the window closed. "We both know the vet said you were at least ten pounds overweight." Though even the vet had admitted the weight was solidly packed. Boo was mostly muscle, not fat.

He gave her one indignant meow, flicked his tail, and headed for the chair by the door. The one Gage had used. Boo jumped on the seat, sniffed the cushions, and curled up with his head on his paws. He blinked twice at Kole then ignored her.

"Great," she muttered. "You're telling me I'm an idiot, aren't you?"

Boo didn't respond. He probably knew he'd made his point.

"Damn, cat. You're supposed to be on *my* side." She walked over and stroked his head. "Well, it just so happens, you're right," she told him. The earthy scents of feline, untamed man, and potion-doctored tea filled her nostrils, turning her thoughts back to Gage. And magnifying the ache in her heart. "I know I'm a fool to love him, Boo. I just don't know what I can do about it."

Chapter 8

48 hours later:

Gage sat at his desk, staring in disbelief at the lab report on the potions he'd sent to be tested. All of them had more beneficial ingredients than he would have thought possible, with no harmful herbs at all. And according to the lab tech, none of the herbs Kole used were cheap. So he couldn't even say she was charging too much for her concoctions. Considering what it cost to make the damn things, her prices were more than reasonable.

He'd gone through her books and found that while

she made a profit on each bottle she sold, it wasn't outrageous. So where was the con?

"I don't believe it."

Gage glanced at Jeff's stunned face and grimaced. "What are you bitching about now?" he asked, though he knew exactly what his partner meant.

"You went to Kole's shop." Jeff gestured at the desk. He slapped Gage on the back then pulled up a chair. "You actually went and got some of her potions. Man, I'm so impressed, I'm speechless."

Gage sighed and closed his eyes a moment. "If only that were true."

Jeff chuckled. "Well, maybe speechless isn't the word I want. But, hey, I *am* impressed. Did she cure your headache while you were there?"

"She gave me some potion-laced tea," Gage admitted sheepishly. "And my headache went away." He held up a hand, irritated by Jeff's knowing smile. "But she also had me sit down for a few minutes and close my eyes." And she'd put her hands on him. No. He refused to think about that—or how much he wanted her to do it again. "So the fact that my headache vanished isn't really proof the potions work. It could have been just coincidence."

"Man, you really are a hardass," Jeff said with a sigh. "I don't expect you to admit it, but deep down you have to know what a crock of bull that is." He shook his head. "If a beat cop came to you with the evidence you have on Trillion's Magic Closet, and you were being totally objective—which is something you can't seem to be about Kole—you'd tell the cop his evidence exonerated the woman." Spreading his hands toward the bottles and papers laid out on top of the desk, he continued. "But since it's *your* evidence and it doesn't say what you want it to, it doesn't prove a thing." He stood and glared down at Gage. "You need to wake up, partner."

"Wake up?"

"Yeah. Stop fooling around with trying to prove Kole's a fraud and admit, at least to yourself, what's really going on."

"Oh, is that right? Then tell me, partner," Gage said, crossing his arms over his chest, "just *what* is really going on?"

"Happy to. Not that it'll do any good." Jeff moved around the desk and leaned close to Gage's ear. "You got shot in the heart with Cupid's arrow the minute you looked at Kole Trillion, but you're too stubborn to admit it."

"That's bullshit." Gage fought down his rising panic. "You're out of your frigging mind."

"Then how come you've been so obsessed with her ever since my wedding?"

"If I've been obsessed with anything, it's with her crimes, not the woman herself."

"Uh-huh." Jeff's smile was back, bigger and bolder than before. "And that cute little arrow sticking out of your chest is just the latest fad in body decorations."

The picture Jeff's words painted in Gage's mind was so ridiculous, he laughed. "First you try to get me to believe in magic, now you're telling me some goofy-looking, diaper-clad god has been shooting arrows at me." Feeling someone's eyes on him, he glanced around, but everyone looked busy. At least, he hadn't caught anyone staring. "Give me a break," he continued, turning his attention back to Jeff and lowering his voice. "I stopped believing in garbage like Cupid when I was six. About the same time I wised up to the fact there isn't really a Santa Claus."

"Is that so?" Jeff chuckled. "Well, your denial might be more effective if you didn't have that arrow sticking out of your chest." He fingered a red bottle of love potion. "All I can say is this little number did me a really big favor. Missy's the best thing that ever happened to me. I just wish you could understand that." With a shrug, he walked away.

Gage buried his head in his hands and groaned. He hadn't been shot by Cupid, and he wasn't obsessed with Kole. True, he hadn't been able to stop thinking about her since the night he met her, but that was because her operation violated everything he stood for.

Even as he thought it, he knew he didn't believe it any longer. The proof he'd been so sure he'd find just wasn't there. Her books showed business was good, but she wasn't making enough of a profit to indicate fraud. Unless she had a second set of books. But even if she did, he'd never get a warrant, based on what he had so far. Maybe Jeff was right. Time to give up this crusade, whether it was idiotic or not.

Yeah. Good idea. He'd close Kole's case and turn his attention to something else. Once he did, he'd forget all about Kole Trillion with her soft hands and sexy green eyes. *Stop thinking about her eyes, dammit!*

He looked at the bottles of potion. Might as well shove them in the trash and clear his desk. The red bottle Jeff had been playing with stood apart from the others, so Gage reached for that one first.

As his fingers closed around the bottle, a sharp pain, like a jolt of electricity, shot from his fingertips all the way up to his chest. He jerked his hand back and gripped the arms of his chair until the discomfort passed. Then he checked himself for injuries. None. At least not that he could see.

Warily, he reached for the potion again. But when he touched it this time, there was no pain. "Must have been static electricity," he muttered, picking up the bottle. The label said "Love Potion No. Two-Fourteen." Cute. She'd probably named it after Valentine's Day. Not a bad marketing tool. Well, the woman was clever. He'd give her that.

Warmth spread through him as he pictured Kole's face in his mind, bringing a thrill that filled him with joy. The only time he could ever remember feeling anything like this before was in his senior year in college when he'd fallen in love with Amanda Bronson. Until she'd trampled all over his heart.

So then what he was feeling now was…love.

What the—

The bottle dropped from his nerveless fingers and landed in his lap. No, he told himself, struggling not to panic. It's not possible. He couldn't be feeling love for Kole Trillion. Absolutely not. He rubbed a hand over his face. Maybe it would pass if he just waited.

But after several minutes, it was clear the feeling wasn't going away. He could sense it even through his fear and confusion. How could this have happened?

The love potion? But the bottle wasn't one of the ones he'd sent to the lab. It was still sealed. He hadn't gotten it on his skin. And he certainly hadn't swallowed any. He studied the little glass container with suspicion. Maybe Kole had lied to him, and all he had to do was touch it. But that couldn't be right. He'd held it a half a dozen times since he took it from the shop, and he'd felt nothing abnormal any of those other times.

He stuffed the bottle in his pocket and hurried to the can to wash his hands. Just in case.

Chapter 9

Kole cringed as she watched Gage storm toward her front door. She'd sent Lynn home early because business was slow. Now, she wished she hadn't.

Seeing the look on Gage's face, she knew she'd need a buffer between herself and his anger. Oh well, at least she was alone, and the store wasn't full of customers to hear whatever accusations he intended to hurl at her this time.

Stiffening her spine, she waited, determined not to let him see how much his dislike hurt her. Still, she couldn't quite stop the wince when he slammed the door behind him and stalked toward her. Only her pride kept her upright instead of cowering out of sight behind the counter.

"Good afternoon, Detective," she said, surprised her voice didn't crack. "What can I do for you this time?"

"You can tell me what you did to me," he growled, slapping a hand on the countertop. "And how the hell you did it."

"I'm afraid I don't know what you mean."

"Dammit, woman, I know you did something to me. Now what was it?"

Figuring one out-of-control person in this conversation was already one too many, Kole fought to keep a muzzle on her own temper. "If you could be a bit more specific—"

"Don't give me that wide-eyed, innocent look." He shoved a hand in his pocket and pulled out a little red bottle. "You said this wouldn't work unless the couple already liked each other," he accused, thrusting the bottle at her like a sword. "You said it couldn't take away my choice. Did you lie about that, too?"

"I didn't lie to you about anything." With a sinking heart, she considered the implications of his words. "Look, Detective, if you were foolish enough to drink my love potion with someone you thought you didn't have any affection for and it backfired on you, I don't see how you can hold me responsible for your own stupidity."

"My own—" Closing his eyes, he took several deep breaths. "Let's back up here a minute." He set the potion on the counter. "Is this one of your love potions or not?"

Kole picked up the bottle. "Yes, it appears to be Love Potion Number Two-Fourteen." She checked it over then looked at him in confusion. "And it's still sealed. So you didn't drink this?"

"Of course, I didn't drink it. What kind of fool do you take me for?"

"Then what's the problem?" she asked. "Why do you think it did something to you?"

He threw up his hand in a gesture so filled with baffled male frustration, it might have made her smile—if it hadn't been for the look in his eyes when he stalked around the counter toward her.

"Because," he said, grabbing her by the shoulders, "I suddenly started having all kinds of strange thoughts about you."

"About me?" Her words came out in a squeak. He was much too close to her. "What kind of thoughts?"

He pinned her against the wall. "This kind," he murmured just before his mouth closed over hers.

It was the shock, she told herself, the complete and utter shock that shut off her brain, stilled her protests, and tossed aside her pride. Shock, not passion, that had her arms winding around his neck and her hands fisting in his hair. Not the heavenly feel of his lips moving over hers. Nor the dark, mysterious taste of him—strong and male with a hot burst of temper—a taste she knew she'd remember the rest of her life. A soft moan escaped her as she leaned into his kiss, into him. She was sure the top of her head would blow off at any second.

Chapter 10

Her low, sexy moan nearly destroyed him, and Gage tightened his embrace, pulling her closer. How could he have known she'd taste so sweet? Be so generous? Or feel so right in his arms? So right that he didn't ever want to let her go.

He couldn't understand what was happening to him. All he knew was he wanted—no, needed—her like he'd never needed anything or anyone before.

Needed? That thought had him jerking back and pulling away from her. He didn't need *anyone*. Ever. Especially not her. It wasn't possible.

Stuffing his hands in his pocket so he couldn't

reach for her again, he glared at her. If he hadn't known better, the dazed look on her face would have made him think she was as shocked as he was. But he did know better. She'd set him up for this. Somehow.

"Are you satisfied now?" he demanded. "Is this what you wanted? Me with no pride, no choice but to make a fool of myself over you? You happy now?"

Once again, her eyes iced over. "Look, asshole, you're the one that came storming in here and attacked me. Not the other way around." She wiped a hand across her lips—lips that were swollen from his kiss. "Now take yourself and your stupid accusations and get the hell out of my store before I report you for police brutality."

"I'm not going anywhere until you tell me what you did to make me feel like I'm in—" No, he couldn't say it. Not even to make his case against her would he admit he thought he was in love with her. "Like I'm obsessed with you."

"Fine, stay. But don't complain to me when you wake up on a lily pad."

"If you want me gone," he told her, ignoring the twinge of apprehension her words caused, "then undo what you did to make me feel like this. Do that, and I'm out of your life for good."

Her sigh sounded much too tired and defeated for

one so young. Hearing it, Gage felt like something that had slithered out of a dark and slimy hole. This was turning out all wrong, but he didn't know how to fix it.

"Kole," he pleaded, desperate enough to try changing tactics. "Help me. Please."

Surprise flashed in her eyes, and her face softened. "Very well. I'll do what I can. But I need more information."

"I've told you how I feel. What more do you need to know?"

"Well, to start with, how long have you felt like this?"

He looked at his watch, calculated. "About forty-five minutes."

"And you say this feeling came on you suddenly?"

"Very."

"What's the last thing you remember before you noticed the feeling?"

He pointed at the love potion. "A sharp pain, like an electric shock, that ran from my fingers to my chest when I touched that."

"That makes no sense." She picked up the bottle and wiped her hands over it. "It's not leaking and the seal isn't broken. You said you didn't drink any of it."

"That's right."

Lips pursed, she paced back and forth behind the

counter a moment. "And other than this…what you called your obsession…you have no other symptoms?"

"I can't think of any. Other than the fact that I came in here intending to strangle you and found myself kissing you instead."

Kissed her, hell, he'd nearly swallowed her whole. In one greedy gulp. And he wasn't about to tell her how much he wanted to do it again.

Her lips twitched. His arms ached to hold her.

"All right, then," she said. "What were you doing just before you felt this pain you mentioned?"

"Nothing much. Just sitting at my desk. Looking over my case notes." He thought back. "Oh, and I was talking to Jeff. About you."

"About me? Can you remember what was said?"

Yeah, he could. He just didn't want to repeat it. Not to her. "I doubt that it's relevant."

"You never know what's relevant and what isn't." When he didn't respond, she shrugged. "I can't help you fix the problem until I know what caused it."

"Whatever," he muttered. Keeping his eyes aimed at the floor, he repeated his conversation with Jeff.

At her startled gasp, he glanced up.

Her delicate hands covered her mouth. The blood had drained from her face, leaving it white and filled with shock.

"Kole?" He hurried back to her side, afraid she'd pass out. "What is it?" he asked, nudging her into a chair.

"You mocked Cupid?"

"I did?" He thought about it. "Well, yeah, I suppose I did. But so what? Is he some special god of magic all witches pray to?"

"You mocked Cupid," she repeated in a hushed voice.

"Yes, I believe we've just established that. Now, let's move on."

The color flowed back into her cheeks. He could tell it was fueled by anger.

She shoved him away. "You *fool*!" Pushing out of the chair, she brushed past him and stormed over to the window. When she turned around to face him, her eyes were hot enough to boil water. "You call Cupid a 'diaper-clad, goofy-looking god,' and then you come charging in here and accuse me of putting a spell on you?" She laughed, but it held no humor, only bitterness. "Apparently, Cupid didn't appreciate your comments."

He stared at her. Did she seriously think Cupid was real? "Kole," he said, shaking his head. "You don't really believe—"

"What? That Cupid exists? Of course I do. He's as real as you and me."

Her eyes dared him to disagree, but he figured he'd gotten himself in enough trouble already and held his tongue. But she obviously wasn't fooled.

She snorted. "Yes, I know. You think there's no such thing as Cupid." She flicked her hand at him, and he felt himself rise off the floor. His mouth dropped open. Another flick and a book sailed off a shelf and smacked him in the head. "Just like there's no such thing as magic."

"What—how?" he stammered as Kole crossed her arms over her chest and smirked at him. He stretched, wiggled, swung his arms and legs, but couldn't lower himself an inch. "Put me down," he snarled. It had to be a trick, he decided, feeling around for a wire. "Dammit, Kole. Put. Me. Down."

"No, I don't think so. I figure if I leave you dangling long enough, eventually you'll have to give up and admit what's right in front of your eyes. And you'll finally have to accept there are some things that can't be explained by cold, hard logic and scientific data." Her finger twitched and another book bonked him on the head.

"Cut that out, dammit." Gage struggled and cursed. Cursed and struggled. It made no difference. "All right, all right. I'm convinced," he finally conceded, knowing he had no choice. "You're a witch, not a fraud. Magic exists, and Cupid is real. There. Happy now?"

"And you agree that I didn't put any kind of spell on you?"

"I suppose I have to, don't I?"

"You're such a gracious loser, Gage." She waved her hand and lowered him to the floor.

He waited until she'd put her hands at her sides before he breathed a sigh of relief and dared to speak. "So Cupid shot me with an arrow because I insulted him? And making me fall for you was…what? My punishment?"

The words no sooner left his mouth than he wanted to call them back. He cursed himself when tears filled her eyes and spilled onto her cheeks.

"Geeze, Kole, I'm sorry," he said helplessly and reached for her. "I didn't mean that like it sounded."

"Don't touch me," she snapped, backing away. "Just get out of my shop and let me be."

"I'm not leaving until you undo whatever was done to me."

She shook her head. "I can't."

"Can't or won't?"

"I can't," she repeated. She wiped the tears off her cheeks and skewered him with a look. "Believe me, if I could undo it, I would. Do you honestly think I'd want someone to be forced to love me against their will? Just how pathetic do you think I am?" The pain in her eyes cut him to the core. "Never mind," she continued. "It doesn't matter what you think." Tucking her hair behind her ears, she took a deep breath. "Trust me, I've got way too much pride to settle for that kind of love, Detective. But, unfortunately, I have no influence over Cupid. Nor am I powerful enough to design a spell or potion that can undo the effects of his arrow. He's a god, and I'm just a lowly witch." She turned away. "Now if you'll excuse me."

"So what the hell I am supposed to do?" he demanded.

"Suffer," she said with a kind of quiet dignity. "Just like me."

Chapter 11

Ten days later:

"You don't have to do this."

"But I want to." Kole looked up from the box she was packing and chuckled at Lynn's hangdog expression. "You'll be fine. You know the products and the customers, and you could manage this store blindfolded. You don't need me."

"That doesn't mean I want you to leave. I'd rather have you here than have you give me a promotion and move away." She draped an arm over Kole's shoulder. "Please don't go. Don't let him chase you away."

Kole stiffened. "Now you're being ridiculous. You can't blame *everything* that happens on Detective Corwin." She pulled out of Lynn's embrace and turned away. Grabbing the picture of her nephews off her desk, she wrapped it in newspaper and packed it in the box. "It's time for me to expand, that's all. Opening a store in Oregon makes good business sense."

"And the fact that *he* suddenly stopped coming around has absolutely no influence on your decision?"

Gage had everything to do with it, but Kole wasn't about to admit it. To anyone. "I thought you wanted him gone," she hedged. "So now that he is, you're complaining?"

"I just find it strange that he spent so much time hanging around the store and investigating you, and then he suddenly disappears into thin air."

Exasperated with Lynn's tenacity, Kole shook her head and evaded the issue. "I'm sure nothing dire has happened to him," she said. "If it had, we'd have heard about it on the news. But since we haven't, I can only assume he's finished his investigation of me and decided he didn't have any evidence that would stick." She took a deep breath. "So he's moved on to his other cases." And taken her heart with him. "We should be grateful he—"

The bell over the front door jingled.

"It sounds like we have a customer." Kole closed her eyes a moment to steel her heart against the stab of hope it was a certain gruff detective and not just a random patron or curious tourist. But no, it wouldn't be Gage. He'd be fighting what he felt for her with everything he had. So her shop was the last place he'd come. How she wished she had his iron-hard control.

Unable to face dealing with the public at the moment, she shot Lynn a pleading look. "Would you mind going out to see what they need?"

"Sure. No problem."

When Lynn left the office, Kole sank into the chair behind the desk. She knew she was running away. She also knew Oregon wouldn't be nearly far enough to let her forget Gage. But at least up there, she wouldn't have to deal with the heart-wrenching burst of anticipation she felt every time the front door opened. Because she wouldn't be foolishly expecting *him* to come through it.

In Oregon, she'd have a new place, one without any reminders of him, or the way he looked the last time he'd left. And maybe up there she wouldn't see his face on every man she encountered. Old or young, short or tall, fat or skinny, the men here were all potentially Gage. In Oregon, they'd just be men. Strangers. Or customers. But she wouldn't jolt at the sight of them, wondering if they might turn out to be him.

At least that was the plan.

She rubbed the grit from her tired eyes then cursed at Boo. He'd jumped up on the desk and was trying to pull items out of the box she'd been packing.

"You don't have to come with me,' she snapped, jerking a handkerchief out of his mouth. "But you're not keeping me from going. So stop trying to unpack for me." Boo batted at her hand then reached a paw into the box and snagged a hairband. She sighed. "Oh, Boo." Retrieving the ribbon, she pulled the huge cat into her arms. "I'm sorry, baby, but I have to go," she whimpered, nuzzling him. "I can't stay here with all this pain."

Tears stung her eyes as Boo cuddled up on her lap, his rumbling purr vibrating her stomach muscles. How she loved this creature. He'd shown up again just minutes after Gage had walked out, and he'd hardly left her side in the ten days since. She knew when it came time to leave California, he'd be right there in the car beside her. Which was a really good thing, since she wasn't sure how she'd survive without him.

"Hey, how's it going?"

Startled by Jeff's voice, she jumped to her feet and sent Boo flying. He hit the floor, hissed at her, flicked his tail, and stalked over to the loveseat under the window.

"Sorry, about that," Jeff said with a sheepish smile. "Lynn said it was okay to come back, but I didn't mean to startle you."

Kole shook her head. "Serves me right for daydreaming instead of working." She dredged up a smile. "It's good to see you. How's Missy?"

"Pregnant." His smile transformed into a grin and spread across his face like a sunrise. "I'm going to be a daddy."

"Oh, Jeff, that's wonderful," she cried, giving him an enthusiastic hug. "I'm so happy for you." She wanted to ask him about Gage, but didn't dare. Blinking away more tears, she tried to make it look like she was misty eyed over Jeff's happy news. "Please tell Missy how thrilled I am for both of you."

"I will." He took her hand and brought to his lips. "It never would've happened without you and your love potion," he said. "So I wanted to come by and say thanks."

Touched, she kissed his cheek. "You're very welcome."

"Missy wanted to come, too, but she's feeling a little peaked right now. Morning sickness."

"Oh. Well, that's easy enough to fix. Grab a few bottles of Stomach Potion One-Twenty-Nine before you leave. Have Missy take a swallow whenever she's nauseous. It'll make her feel better."

"Thanks, I'll do that. So what's going on with you?" He gestured at the packing box on the desk and the pictures she'd taken off the wall and stacked by the door. "Redecorating?"

"No." She managed to keep her voice from breaking. "I'm moving up to Oregon to open another store."

"Oregon?"

At the panic on his face, she smiled. "Don't worry. This store will stay open. Lynn will manage the business here, while I open a shop up there. And you'll still be able to buy all my products online."

"But you'll be gone."

"It's a good business decision, Jeff. And it's time I moved on anyway."

"Uh-huh." Even before he gripped her shoulders, she knew he didn't buy it. "This wouldn't have anything to do with Gage, would it, Kole?"

"Don't be silly." She stepped out from underneath his hands. "Why would you even think that?"

He cocked a brow. "Oh, I don't know. Maybe because for the last ten days Gage has been as grumpy as a grizzly bear with a toothache. Comes to work early, leaves late, and bites the head off anyone who speaks to him. And he absolutely refuses to talk about you." He ran a hand down her arm. "Did anything unusual happen between you?"

"Not exactly." She knew if she didn't give him something, he'd keep prodding until he got everything. He was a cop, after all. "Gage stormed in here ten days ago and started making wild accusations," she told him, deciding on an edited version of the truth. "I'm afraid I lost my temper and gave him a demonstration of magic he couldn't ignore." Her lips twitched in spite of her pain as she remembered the dumbfounded look on Gage's face. "I hung him up in the air then made a couple of books fly across the room and smack him in the head."

Jeff burst out laughing. "You didn't!"

"I most certainly did. And I left him hovering three feet off the floor until he admitted magic existed and I wasn't a fraud." She turned away and continued packing so Jeff couldn't see her face. "He's probably just moving on to his other cases now and trying to make up for lost time." When she was sure she could control her expression, she pasted on a smile and turned back around. "I know you're worried about him, Jeff, but he'll be okay. I imagine he's just angry with himself for wasting so much energy on me."

"Right." Jeff wrapped her in a hug. "Don't go, Kole. Please. Gage will come around. He's a good man.

Really. He's stubborn, but deep down he cares about you. I know he does. He just doesn't want to admit it."

Giving in for a moment, she took the comfort of resting her head against a friendly shoulder. She knew Jeff believed what he said. But he didn't know the whole story, and it wasn't her place to tell him that Cupid's arrow had forced Gage to love her against his will. So it was a love he wasn't willing to share with her. And one she could never accept from him.

Chapter 12

I've got to hand it to you, pal. You really are a first-class bastard."

Gage looked up from his case file, straight into to Jeff's angry face. "What the hell are you whining about now?"

"She's hurting, even though she won't admit it. And I know you had something to do with it."

Gage's heart contracted. A niggle of fear settled in his stomach. "Who are you talking about?" he demanded, even though he was pretty sure he knew. "And what does it have to do with me?"

"I'm talking about Kole, you jerk. I don't know

what you did to make her hurt, but I'm sure it's your fault."

Gage closed his eyes a moment, praying for patience. He was the victim here, not Kole. Yet even as he thought it, he remembered the pain in her voice when she said he'd suffer just like her.

He didn't want to think about her suffering because he couldn't afford to soften. If he did, he'd never be able to stay away from her. As it was, he thought about her during every waking minute and dreamed about her for most of the night—if he could actually get to sleep, that is. But if he saw her again, he'd be lost.

He opened his eyes to find Jeff staring at him, waiting for a response. Gage shrugged, hoping it looked casual. "Even if she *is* hurting, I don't see how you come up with it being my fault."

"Don't you, Gage? Don't you *really*?"

"Look, partner, I did what you asked and gave up my crusade against her. I closed the case and logged it in as a 'no evidence of any wrongdoing.' And I've stayed completely away from her and her shop ever since."

"And that exonerates you, does it? You close the case, and that's it? Your responsibility's over? What about all the pain you caused her?"

"I doubt the investigation hurt her much," Gage

muttered. No, but *he* had, and he knew it. The guilt flooding his mind added a belligerent edge to his voice. "Just what the hell do you want from me? Blood?" He told himself he couldn't afford to feel sorry for her. He had to worry about his own survival. "I even said, 'I'm sorry,' the last time I saw her. So if she's hurting now, it's not my problem."

Jeff slapped his hands down on the desk. "You know, partner, I used to have nothing but respect for you. When you were wrong, you admitted it. If you made a mistake, you tried to fix it. You were someone I could look up to. Hell, I even told Kole you were a good man." He straightened and folded his arms across his chest. "Now, I'm just disappointed in you. Disappointed that a cop I respected could hurt an innocent woman so much she'd pack up and move just to get away from the pain. I can't believe you can look me in the eye and say it's not your problem."

Kole was moving? Shock kept Gage frozen in his chair as Jeff stormed away. It had to be a mistake. She wouldn't pack up and leave her shop and her customers just because he'd hurt her feelings. Would she? And even if she did, why should he care? He should be relieved she was moving. Then he wouldn't have to worry about running into her by accident. It'd be easier to deal with what Cupid had done to him that way.

So why was it panic churning in his gut and not relief? And why did it seem the only thing in his miserable life that really mattered was about to slip through his fingers?

He told himself the feelings he had for Kole weren't really his. They'd been artificially implanted by an obnoxious little god with a magic arrow. They were just an illusion. They couldn't bring him real happiness. Hell, he hadn't had a moment's contentment since…

The realization stunned him. The last time he'd felt any kind of joy, or even peace, was for a few brief moments when he first discovered he was in love with Kole. And the one time he'd kissed her, when she felt so right in his arms, like she'd always belonged there. Always belonged to him. She'd brought him happiness—when she responded to his kiss, when she treated his headache. When she'd touched him and given him tea. When she smiled.

She was honest, warm, generous, loyal, and compassionate. In fact, she was everything he'd ever wanted. In a moment of perfect clarity, he knew he'd loved her from the moment he saw her at Jeff's wedding. Her laugh had reached him from across the room and filled him with joy. Before he'd known who she was, he'd recognized the light in her eyes and the warmth in her smile as the result of a loving and generous heart.

So it had been a crushing disappointment to find out she was none other than the woman who'd helped Missy con Jeff. But had she really? Jeff was going to be a father, and the happiness was bouncing off him in waves. And Missy was suffering from morning sickness. Suddenly, it didn't look like a con at all.

Oh no, what have I done? Horrified, Gage dropped his head into his hands. He'd accused and harassed an innocent woman just because she didn't fit into what he considered the norm. Because he hadn't believed in what she was. Even after she helped him, he'd given her nothing but grief.

Then when he'd been shot with Cupid's arrow—his own fault, not Kole's—his response had been to accuse her of lying and call loving her a punishment. A punishment! Geeze, how much more insulting could he have been?

Maybe she was a witch, but she loved him. Despite all he'd done, she loved him. He'd known it by the way she'd returned his kiss. And even knowing it, he'd still heaped more pain on her.

Jeff was right. He really was a bastard.

Now she was leaving, and he'd lose her forever. He grabbed his keys. Moving, huh? Like hell, she was!

Chapter 13

"Where is she?" Gage's angry words echoed through the shop.

Out of sight in her office, Kole closed her eyes and groaned. It was a good thing they didn't have any customers in the shop at the moment.

"You don't have to shout, Detective." Lynn's voice dripped with hostility. "As you can see, she isn't here. Is there something I can help you with? Would you like another headache potion? Maybe some hemlock-laced tea?"

"I want to know where Kole is."

"People in Hell want ice water, but I can't help them, either."

Kole stifled a giggle then bit her lip. Geeze, what did the man want with her now? She knew she was acting like a coward, hiding in here. But if Lynn could get rid of him so Kole wouldn't have to face him, maybe she could get out of town without having her heart shredded. Again. She'd had her quota of emotional anguish from the man and didn't relish any more.

The thought had barely formed in her mind when Boo jumped up on the desk. He head-butted the lamp and knocked it over the edge. Kole grabbed for it but missed. It shattered on impact with the floor, making a tremendous crash.

Footsteps thundered toward the office.

"Traitor," she hissed at Boo as Lynn and Gage appeared in the office doorway. "It's nothing," she told them, glaring at the cat. "Boo just had a little accident."

Boo hopped off the desk and sauntered out the office door. *Nice. He accomplishes his treachery then leaves me to deal with the aftermath. Great job, Boo. Thanks a lot.*

Knowing it was pointless to pretend she hadn't heard Gage and Lynn, Kole took a deep breath. "You wanted to see me, Detective?"

"Yeah," he said. "We need to talk."

The gruffness in his voice made her sigh. She wasn't looking forward to this.

Lynn stamped her foot. "Now, look, Detective—"

Kole patted her on the arm. "It's all right. I'll be fine. If you could watch the store while I speak with Detective Corwin, I'd appreciate it."

"Yeah, we'd appreciate it," Gage repeated, shutting the door in Lynn's face.

"Honestly, Detective. Is it really necessary for you to be so rude?"

"Yeah." He jammed his hands into his pockets. "More often than you'd think."

"Whatever." Uncomfortable with the way he was looking at her, and wanting to keep her hands busy, she pulled the broom out of the closet and began cleaning up Boo's mess. When Gage didn't speak, she glanced up. "You wanted to talk, so talk."

"I'm sorry."

She blinked. "Excuse me?"

With a groan of frustration, Gage pulled his hands out of his pockets and raked them through his hair. "Geeze, Kole. I said, I'm sorry, dammit!"

What the hell was this? He was *sorry*? After everything he'd done, everything he'd said, did he really think those two words, "I'm sorry," cleared the slate? Probably.

And if she'd had a lick of common sense, they would have. She should let it be enough, just accept it, smile, tell him she understood, and then make him leave. But her stubborn pride wouldn't let her.

"Let me get this straight," she said slowly. "You came here to apologize? And you do this how? By swearing at me?" Shaking her head, she reached in the closet for the dustpan. "I have to admit, I've never had an apology quite like it before. I imagine it's a fairly unique approach."

He surprised her by laughing. "Yeah, I guess it is." Stepping toward her, he took the broom and dustpan and set them aside. His hands came down on her shoulders as he backed her against the desk. "Okay then," he murmured. "Let's try it this way." And he brought his mouth crushing down on hers.

As apologies went, she decided as her bones started to melt, this one wasn't half bad. When he changed the angle of the kiss and took her deeper, she went willingly. She slipped her arms around his neck and pressed herself against him, her mouth every bit as greedy as his.

The earthy scent of untamed male filled her nostrils and his taste—that dark, erotic flavor of strength and passion—danced on her tongue. She heard her soft, desperate moan, felt it in her throat.

He broke the kiss and ran his lips over her face. "Damn, Kole," he groaned, burying his face in her hair.

"You can't imagine how much I needed this. It's been a very long ten days."

Chapter 14

'*Ten days*.' The words were like a slap in the face. What on earth was she doing? What was she thinking? Gage was acting on feelings he'd had no choice in. Feelings Cupid had given him that he didn't even want. If she lost control of her own emotions, she'd never have the strength to leave. With rising panic, she pushed him away.

"Enough," she gasped. She wiped the back of her hand over her mouth as she caught her breath. "Apology accepted. Now it's time for you to go."

He winced, but his eyes hardened. "Not until you hear me out."

"What more is there to say?" She had to get him out of her office—correction, her life—before she broke down completely. "You've apologized. I've forgiven you. We should be done here."

"You've forgiven me, huh?" His laugh was short and bitter. "Somehow, I doubt that."

Desperate to make him leave, she tried again. "Look, I understand that you didn't believe in magic before, and you thought I was a con artist. Naturally, you considered it your moral obligation to investigate me since you suspected I was cheating the public. And I can even see how you'd think Cupid was punishing you when he—" Pain sliced through her as she remembered Gage's words. She swallowed then gritted her teeth and continued. "—when he did what he did to you. So yes, I really do forgive you."

A wicked gleam leapt into his eyes, and her hands shot up.

"No, don't get any ideas. Just stay where you are and listen." She took a deep breath. "I'm also very aware that you don't want to feel any affection for me."

"Kole, I should never have—"

"I don't blame you for that. In fact, I sympathize completely. I'd be furious if I was forced to love someone against my will."

"But it's not against my—"

"No, really. It's all right. Please don't think you have to spare my feelings."

"Dammit, woman, if you'd let me finish a sentence!"

She fought a quick, but fierce, internal war with her temper, bit back her sarcastic remarks before they could slip out, and nodded.

Gage sighed then scooped his hands through his hair again. "Look," he said. "I know I've never given you any reason to trust me, but please believe I'm giving it to you straight here." He flexed his hands as if he was going to reach for her but shoved them back into his pockets instead. "You're right that I was upset and angry when you told me I got shot by Cupid." When she opened her mouth, he cocked his head and raised an eyebrow, so she kept quiet. "That's '*was* upset and angry,'" he went on. "Past tense. I've done considerable thinking since Jeff told me you were moving, and I've come to some startling conclusions. One." Freeing his hands from his pockets again, he tapped his left index finger with his right. "I've been wrong about you from the beginning. And I'm really very sorry for that. Two." He tapped another finger. "Cupid didn't make me feel what I do for you." He gently cupped her face with his hands. "I began feeling it the minute I heard you laugh and spied you across the room at Jeff's wedding."

She stared at him. "But you said—when you—" Hearing herself stutter, she stopped and started over. "When you came to the shop that afternoon, you said it happened all of a sudden."

"That's point number three," he said. "The strength of what I felt when I first saw you was unexpected. It scared me. I panicked and convinced myself it was a plot, and you and Missy were in on it together." He kissed her forehead then her eyelids. "I'm not proud of it. And I guess I owe Missy an apology as well." His lips brushed hers. "But you come first. I don't want to lose you, Kole."

She wrapped her arms around him, floating on his words and the scent and feel of his body. "So then Cupid didn't shoot you?"

"Hmm? Oh. Yeah, I guess he must have. But what difference does it make?"

The bubble of happiness she'd been drifting on popped and sent her crashing back to earth. Good heavens, she'd almost surrendered to him. "What *difference* does it make?" she demanded, pushing him away. "It makes *all* the difference. Do you think I'm so pathetic I can't get a man without Cupid's help?" The anger eased the pain of her heartbreak, so she let herself ride the crest. "Or maybe you think I put him up to it, that I'd be willing to accept the love of a man who had no choice. That I *could* accept it."

"Of course I don't think that."

"Well, that's good, because I didn't, I won't, and I can't."

"It's not like that," he shouted. "I love you. And unless I'm very much mistaken, you love me, too."

It wasn't hard to work up some outrage to go with her anger. "*Excuse* me?"

"Don't look at me that way." He shot her a cocky grin. "Come on, admit it. I know you're crazy about me."

No. He couldn't know that. Not for sure. He had to be fishing. Bluffing, in hopes she'd confess. So he thought his cop tactics would work on her, did he?

"If you think I'd fall for an arrogant, conceited, self-absorbed—" She couldn't think of anything else bad enough, so she settled for shaking her head and glaring.

"Yeah, I'm all that and more, but you love me anyway."

"You're out of your mind." She strode to the door and flung it open. "Now, you listen to me. You need to go. Right now. I'm leaving for Oregon tonight." She started across the threshold ahead of him. "And I'm way behind schedule."

"Oregon? The hell you are!" He grabbed her arm and pulled her back into the office. "You're not going anywhere."

She snorted. "I'm a witch, Gage. Do you really think you can stop me from leaving?" When he nodded, she smiled. "I'd like to see you try." She tossed her head and straightened her spine. "How'd you like to hang in the air again and dodge books for a while?"

"Oh no, you don't." As she started to raise her hand, he grabbed both wrists and held her arms at her sides, resting his forehead on hers. "How about we compromise instead?"

"What kind of compromise?" she asked, suspicious of the way he was grinning.

"Wait right here. I'll get it."

"Get what?"

But he'd already darted into the shop. When he came back, he had a bright red bottle of Love Potion No. Two-Fourteen.

"Okay, here's the deal. You drink this little bottle of potion. And if, after the seventy-two hours are up, you still claim you don't love me, you can head for Oregon." He closed and locked the office door then handed her the bottle. "I promise I won't try to stop you."

"You want me to drink this? To prove I don't love you?"

"Yeah. What's the matter? You afraid?"

"Why should I be?" Damn right, she was. The potion would be her undoing. She wouldn't stand a chance against him. "I just don't see why I should waste three whole days."

"Let me put it this way, Kole." He leaned against the door and glared at her. "If you don't do this, then even if you do manage to get to Oregon, I'll follow you there and make your life hell until you give in."

"You wouldn't dare!"

"Oh, yeah? Try me."

"Wait." She had to think of something to dissuade him. What about a forgetfulness potion? She hadn't considered it before because it was only intended for people who'd lost a loved one and were suffering from unnatural, debilitating grief. But there wasn't any *real* reason she couldn't use it on Gage. Besides, she was desperate. "What if I could give you a potion?" she asked. "One that would make you forget all about me, despite what Cupid did to you?"

"Not interested," he growled. "I want to be in love with you."

"You *what*?"

He kissed her—gently this time. "Remember those conclusions I mentioned earlier?" he asked, nibbling on her lips. "One of them was that the only times I've felt any kind of peace or happiness was when I'm with you. And when I realized I loved you." Sliding his arms around her, he pulled her closer and nuzzled her neck. She trembled. "I don't want to lose that feeling. I don't want to lose you." He tightened his embrace and gave her a long, drugging kiss. "Take the potion, Kole. In fact, we'll both take it. I love you. And I don't regret it. Don't throw that away just because I've been an idiot."

She heard the desperation in his voice and felt herself weakening.

"Let's drink your magic brew, my beautiful little witch," he pleaded. "And take the chance that comes with it. What have we got to lose?"

"You really mean that?" She stared into his eyes and saw the answer she needed.

"More than I've ever meant anything in my life."

"That's good, because you were right. I do love you, Gage." A joyful laugh bubbled up out of her throat as she set the bottle on the desk. "We can take the potion if you really want to." She threw her arms around him. Held on tight. "But I don't think we're going to need it."

He laughed. "Perhaps not." Scooping her up, he crossed to the loveseat. He lowered her to the cushions as his fingers went to work on the buttons of her blouse. "I suppose we can try it this way first."

About the Author

Award-winning author, Pepper O'Neal is a researcher, a writer, and an adrenaline junkie. She has a doctorate in education and spent several years in Mexico and the Caribbean working as researcher for an educational resource firm based out of Mexico City. During that time, she met and befriended many adventurers like herself, including former CIA officers and members of organized crime. Her fiction is heavily influenced by the stories they shared with her, as well her own experiences abroad.

O'Neal attributes both her love of adventure and her compulsion to write fiction to her Irish and Cherokee ancestors. When she's not at her computer, O'Neal spends her time taking long walks in the forests near her home or playing with her cats. And of course, planning the next adventure.

Visit Pepper at: www.pepperoneal.com